THE
ONE & ONLY
GOOGOOSH

IRAN'S BELOVED SUPERSTAR

AZADEH WESTERGAARD

VIKING

You were two when you first appeared onstage,
and your acrobat father pulled you out of his trouser cuffs
like a rosebud plucked fresh from the vine—
introducing us to the one and only Googoosh.

While we rode our tricycles around our garden ponds,
you swung from your father's arms
like the ticktock of a clock.
While we dangled from the tips of the tallest trees,
you climbed atop a ladder of chairs—
balanced on your father's chin.

And while we sat in classrooms reciting the alphabet,
you stood backstage, mimicking our favorite musicians—
your voice turning like a radio knob
between the trills of the sopranos
and the booming bellows of the baritones.

You were four when you first sang onstage—
so small, you needed a step stool to reach the microphone.
And as we watched you, we wondered:
How can one child sing with so much feeling?

As word of your talent spread,
we gathered in larger and larger crowds—

the rhythm of your music swelling in our hearts
like the waves of our beloved Caspian Sea,
your voice, like the warbling bolbols that woke us at dawn.

Like the snowcapped peaks of the Alborz Mountains,
you were everywhere we turned
as we twisted and twirled to dance like you

and cut and colored our hair to look like you—
even though we knew no one could compare
to our one and only Googoosh.

But then one day,
   as our steaming samovars steeped the morning tea,
   as our bakers sold warm barbari bread
   straight from their wood-fired tanoors

and street vendors peddled
fresh-squeezed pomegranate juice
and salted boiled beets—

life as we knew it changed forever.

Concert halls were shuttered.
Your recordings and posters, destroyed.
And the sound of a woman's singing voice—
outlawed.

You were given no choice but to step offstage
and agree to never perform in public again.

And just like that,
you and us,
we, together—
amidst the roar and thunder of a revolution
that turned our country into a typhoon of turmoil—
lost the only home we knew.

While you and so many chose to stay,
the rest of us fled,
eager for freedom and scared for our safety—
scattering across the world
like wild, windblown poppies.

With our overstuffed suitcases, hastily packed,
and handkerchiefs damp with goodbyes,
your melodies traveled with us
over the Alborz Mountains and across the Caspian Sea,

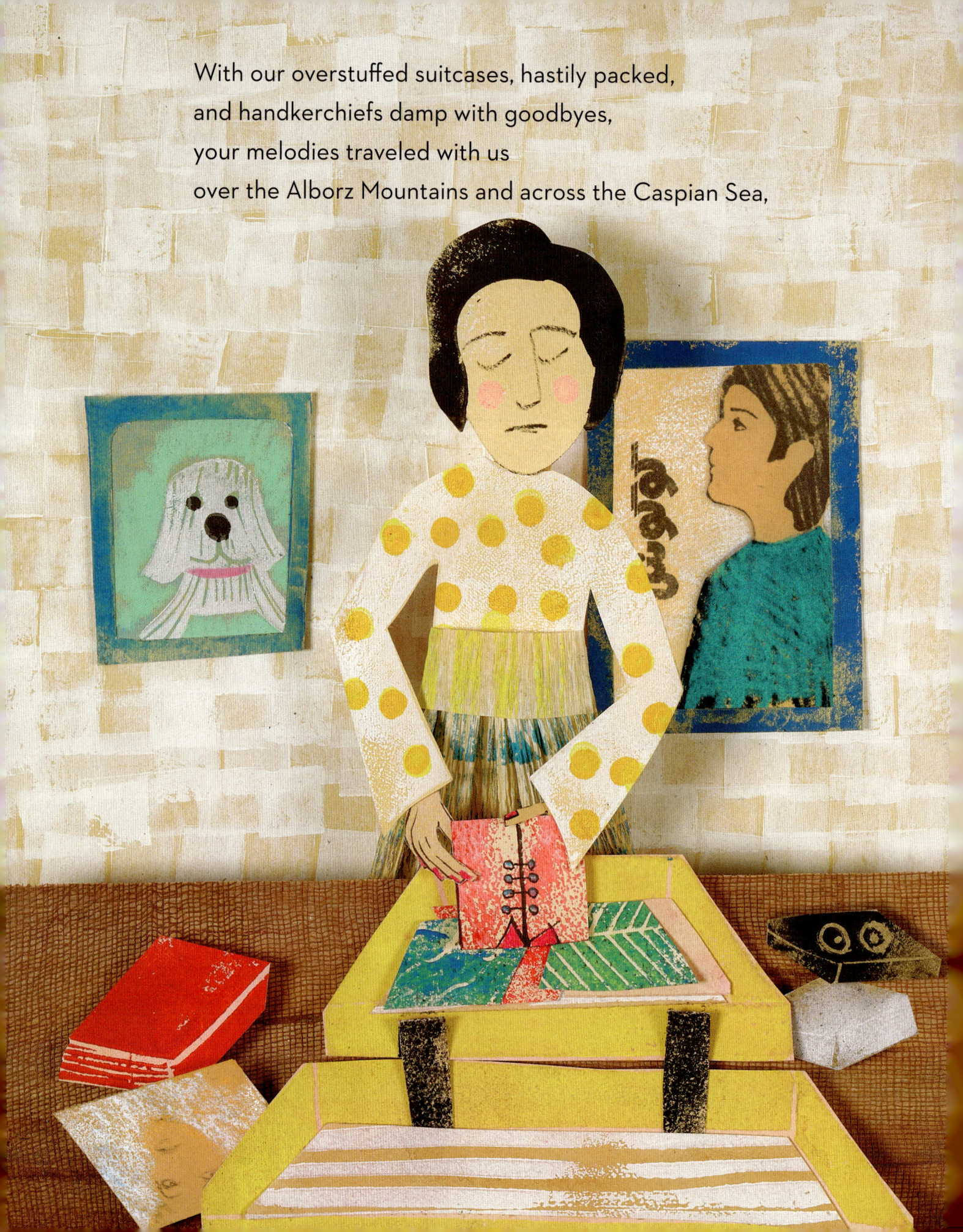

hiding inside cassettes spooled with ribbons
that preserved your music—
a witness to what once was.

And in our far-flung kitchens, still fragrant with the scents
of slow-simmering stews and steaming saffron rice,
your songs stayed alive on our lips,
marking our milestones and our day-to-day,
forever pressed in our memories—
sweet like the taste of our grandmother's halva,
tender like the soft touch of her farewell kiss.

Your silence spoke louder than any song
as the years slipped through our fingers
like the stringed prayer beads
our grandfathers used to mark time.

We didn't know that offstage,
you stepped into darkness
and began a new life—
quietly tending to tasks of the everyday
while finding solace in Hafez and Rumi's rhymes.

When at last you were able
to travel to a country where women
were free to sing alone onstage,

we, some now frail and gray with age,
traveled in haste
across the world's oceans and mountains
to bear witness to your return.

And on the night of our reunion,
as twelve thousand of us sat in our seats,
when the curtains opened
and you stepped back onstage—

our tears spoke louder than any song.

Then when you finally sang,
and the ribbons of memory unspooled around our feet,
we were all together again
in our homeland, Iran—

where the bolbols still warble at dawn,
where the Caspian Sea still swells with sturgeon,
and where snow still powders the peaks of the Alborz Mountains.

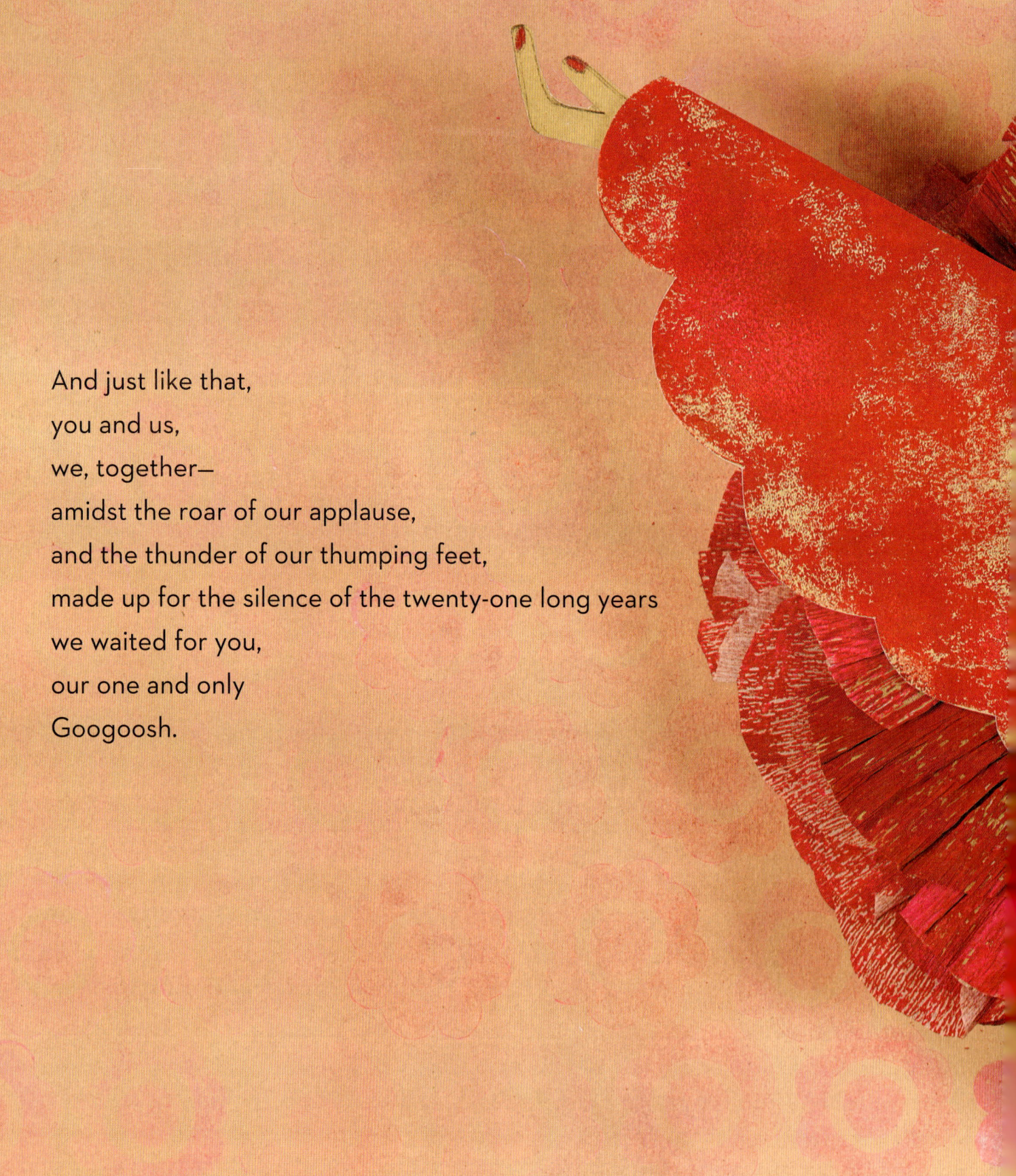

And just like that,
you and us,
we, together—
amidst the roar of our applause,
and the thunder of our thumping feet,
made up for the silence of the twenty-one long years
we waited for you,
our one and only
Googoosh.